W9-ATZ-179

Dear Parent:
Your child's love of reading starts here!

I Can Read Books have introduced children to the joy of reading since 1957. Featuring award-winning authors and illustrators and a fabulous cast of beloved characters, I Can Read Books set the standard for beginning readers. From books your child reads with you to the first books they read alone, there are I Can Read Books for every stage of reading:

SHARED READING
Basic language, word repetition, and whimsical illustrations, ideal for sharing with your emergent reader

BEGINNING READING
Short sentences, familiar words, and simple concepts for children eager to read on their own

READING WITH HELP
Engaging stories, longer sentences, and language play for developing readers

READING ALONE
Complex plots, challenging vocabulary, and high-interest topics for the independent reader

ADVANCED READING
Short paragraphs, chapters, and exciting themes for the perfect bridge to chapter books

Every child learns in a different way and at their own speed. Some read through each level in order. Others go back and forth between levels and read favorite books again and again. You can help your young reader improve and become more confident by encouraging their own interests and abilities.

A lifetime of discovery begins with the magical words, **"I Can Read!"**

For Erica and Laura—
city mouse, country mouse!
—A.S.C.

No part of this publication may be reproduced, stored in a retrieval system, or transmitted in any form or by any means, electronic, mechanical, photocopying, recording, or otherwise, without written permission of the publisher. For information regarding permission, write to HarperCollins Children's Books, a division of HarperCollins Publishers, 1350 Avenue of the Americas, New York, NY 10019.

ISBN-13: 978-0-439-91763-6
ISBN-10: 0-439-91763-8

Text copyright © 2006 by Alyssa Satin Capucilli.
Illustrations copyright © 2006 by Pat Schories. All rights reserved.
Published by Scholastic Inc., 557 Broadway, New York, NY 10012, by arrangement with HarperCollins Children's Books, a division of HarperCollins Publishers. I Can Read Book® is a trademark of HarperCollins Publishers Inc. SCHOLASTIC and associated logos are trademarks and/or registered trademarks of Scholastic Inc.

12 11 10 9 8 7 6 5 4 3 2   7 8 9 10 11 12/0

Printed in the U.S.A.   23

First Scholastic printing, January 2007

MY FIRST
I Can Read Book®

Biscuit Visits the Big City

story by ALYSSA SATIN CAPUCILLI
pictures by PAT SCHORIES

SCHOLASTIC INC.
New York   Toronto   London   Auckland   Sydney
Mexico City   New Delhi   Hong Kong   Buenos Aires

Here we are, Biscuit.

Woof, woof!

We're in the big city.

We're going to visit
our friend Jack.

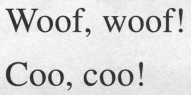

Woof, woof!

Coo, coo!

Stay with me, Biscuit.

It's very busy in the big city!

Woof, woof!

There are lots of tall buildings
in the big city, Biscuit.
Woof, woof!

There are lots of people, too.
Woof, woof!

Funny puppy!
You want to say hello
to everyone.

Stay with me, Biscuit.

It's very busy here!

Woof, woof!

Beep! Beep!

Woof!

It's only a big bus, Biscuit.

Woof, woof!

You found the fountain,
Biscuit.

There's so much to see
in the big city,
isn't there, Biscuit?

Woof!

Coo, coo!

Woof, woof!
Coo, coo!

Woof, woof! Woof, woof!

Oh no, Biscuit! Come back!

Biscuit, where are you going?

Woof!

Silly puppy! Here you are.

This is a big, busy city, Biscuit.
But you found our friend Jack,
and some new friends, too!

Coo, coo!

Woof!